Yum, Apples!

written by Tina Athaide
illustrated by Farah Aria

Bebop Books
An imprint of LEE & LOW BOOKS Inc.

This is a seed.

It grows and grows.

This is a tree.

It grows and grows.

This is a bud.

It grows and grows.

This is a flower.

It grows and grows.

This is an apple.

It grows and grows.

Yum, apples!